ANANSI and the GOLDEN POT

Taiye Selasi

For my Safa, the most marvelous of storytellers.

Illustrated by **Tinuke Fagborun**

There was once a little boy whose name was Kweku, but everyone called him **Anansi**.
Anansi's father, Kojo, picked the nickname.

"In Ghana," said Kojo, "where I was born, everyone knows Anansi—a clever little spider with a sparkle in his eye."

Anansi's eyes were sparkly too, with spider leg-like lashes.
Anansi loved his nickname, and he loved those spidery lashes.

He especially loved the traditional tales
his parents told at bedtime—stories
of the adventures of one little
trickster spider.

Then, one winter, Anansi
had an adventure of his own.

From the cold of the city he flew to the warmth of the beach where his father was born.

Of course, Anansi's sister and brother—Amma and Ato—came, too.

Anansi's nana was waiting to greet
them. Anansi adored his nana.
Wise and kind, she had sparkly
eyes and spidery lashes as well.

Vacations on the beach!
What joy!
There were so many things to do...

Anansi climbed the coconut trees and drank the cool, sweet water.

He hauled in nets with fishermen. He helped his nana cook.

Anansi's favorite thing was to eat Nana's red-red, a stew of beans, with fried plantain— the greatest joy of all.

Then, one day, a stranger appeared
—this is, after all, an adventure.
Sipping a coconut, shaded by palms,
Anansi felt legs crawling on his head!
Eight skinny legs, to be exact.

"Eeek!" he cried. "A spider!"
"Observant," said a soft—and rather
mischievous—little voice.

The spider leapt from Anansi's
head and down into his hand.
"Allow me to introduce myself."
But he needed no introduction.

"Anansi the spider!"
said Anansi the boy.
"So my bedtime stories were true!"

"Traditional stories are always true,"
the spider answered, laughing.
"Nothing lasts so long as truth,
nor travels quite so far."

"See that pot?"
the spider continued.
Anansi looked around them.

All he saw were the empty shells
of coconuts on the ground.
"All I see are coconuts,"
Anansi said, perplexed.

The spider merely chuckled. "Observant," he said again.
Then he hopped from Anansi's hand and scurried to a shell.
"This, my boy, is a **golden pot**."

It was Anansi's turn to laugh.
"But that's a coconut shell,"
Anansi chuckled, showing
the spider. **"Look!"**

"I didn't say *look*," the spider said, impatient.

"I said see."

Anansi turned the shell in his hands.
And then, indeed, he saw: the inside
of the coconut shell was bright
and sparkling gold!

The spider winked.

"As I said. A golden pot. See?"
He crawled up Anansi's
leg, which tickled, and
onto Anansi's shoulder,
from where he could
whisper in Anansi's ear.

"And now for the fun part.

MAGIC!"

"Close your eyes and repeat these words," the spider instructed Anansi.

"Do for me as you do for Spider!

Fill with what I most desire!"

And closing his eyes, cupping the pot, Anansi repeated the charm.

No sooner had Anansi spoken than the smell of ginger filled his nose. He opened his eyes and saw: the pot had filled with red-red stew! The entire shell was golden now. A magic golden pot!

"A golden pot for a golden heart," the spider said, and winked. "Just remember. You must share what you love with those you love the most."

"I will!" said Anansi, mouth full of red-red.
But, alas, he didn't.

In the days that followed,
Anansi kept the golden
pot by his side.

Splashing in the ocean...

taking a bath...

building castles
from sand.

Whenever he
craved his favorite
food, he spoke the
spider's charm.

"Do for me as you do for Spider!
Fill with what I most desire!"

However, he kept the pot a secret from Amma and Ato, afraid that they would steal it.

He didn't even tell Nana. Anansi feasted alone.

All he could eat! All for himself! Or rather: all *by* himself.

In truth, Anansi grew lonely, hiding from Nana and Amma and Ato. Hiding the golden pot beneath his pillow made his head hurt. Not to mention his tummy—red-red is made of beans after all!

One night, Nana—who, after all,
was wise as well as kind—sat on
the edge of Anansi's bed, rubbing
his aching tummy.

"When I was young...," Nana began.
"But you're *still* young," objected Anansi.

"In spirit, yes," laughed Nana.
"But when I was *also* young in body... my parents
told me tales about a spider and his pot.
The stories were always different but the
lesson was the same."

A very sleepy Anansi asked, although
he suspected he already knew,
"What was the lesson?"

"Greed brings grief.
Generosity brings **joy**."

In the morning Anansi found Amma and Ato, and showed them the golden pot.

"What is *that*?!" They gasped with wonder. Anansi closed his eyes.

"Do for me as you do for Spider! Fill with what I most desire!"

This time, however, instead
of filling with his favorite food,
the golden pot filled with Amma's
favorite—**kelewele**—then
Ato's favorite—**ice cream**.

Amma and Ato ate with delight.
And Anansi watched,
delighted.

Now he felt something on his neck. Eight skinny legs. Which tickled.

Then he felt something in his heart.

Generosity.
Which glowed.

"You must share what you love," the spider began, but Anansi finished for him.
"With those you love the most," Anansi said, and laughed with joy.

Learn more about the story...

Ghana is a country in West Africa. This is where, centuries ago, the character of Anansi the Spider was born. No one knows who invented Anansi, but we do know he first appeared in stories told by the Akan people in the Ashanti region of Ghana. In traditional stories, Anansi the Spider is a "trickster," which is a person who fools others to get what they want (but never to harm them, of course).

"Anansi" means "spider" in the Akan language.

Ashanti Region

Anansi stories traveled in the hearts of storytellers from West Africa to the Americas, Europe... and now to you! You are part of a wonderful web. Where will you take Anansi next?

So, how did a centuries-old tale get from Ghana to you?
In Ghana, stories were traditionally spoken aloud rather than written down. Because the same few stories were told lots of times, everyone knew them by heart. A written story can get lost or destroyed. A spoken story cannot. This is why tales of Anansi the Spider have lasted for so long.

If you had a magic golden pot, what would you fill it with?

Bofrot (Bow-froat)

A delicious fried pastry that can be served as a snack.

Waakye (Waa-chay)

A Ghanaian dish that is served with a tomato stew. Waakye is made with rice, beans, and a special leaf.

Fruit

Sugarloaf pineapples, mango, and papaya are delicious tropical fruits grown in Ghana.

Jollof (Joh-luff)

A West African dish made with rice, tomatoes, onions, and spices.

Kenkey (Ken-kay)

Kenkey is a type of sour dumpling made from steamed white corn. It is served wrapped in corn husks.

Sugarcane

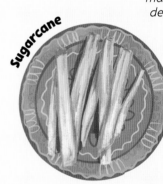

Sugarcane is a type of grass, from which we get... sugar! Chewing on a stick of sugarcane releases sweet liquid. Yum!

Kelewele (Keh-leh-weh-leh)

Sliced fried plantain seasoned with ginger and spices.

Adinkra are symbols from Ghana that represent concepts. Can you spot these ones throughout the book?

Ananse Ntontan
"spider's web".
A symbol of wisdom and creativity.

Nea Onnim No Sua A, Ohu
"he who does not know can know from learning".
A symbol of knowledge wisdom and creativity.

Nkyinkyim
"twisting". A symbol of initiative, dynamism and versatility.

Ese Ne Tekrema
"the teeth and the tongue". A symbol of friendship and interdependence.

Taiye Selasi

Taiye Selasi is a novelist and screenwriter of Nigerian and Ghanaian origin. Taiye's true love is storytelling. As a child, Taiye loved West African fables and as soon as she could grip a pen she started writing her own. To pass this passion on to other children who love books brings Taiye boundless joy.

Tinuke Fagborun

Tinuke Fagborun is a London-based, northern-born, British-Nigerian illustrator. As a child, Tinuke always had a sketchbook and paintbrush in hand. Her style developed over time to incorporate her Nigerian heritage, borrowing from its rich history, colorful textiles, and intricate patterns.

DK | Penguin Random House

Author Taiye Selasi
Illustrator Tinuke Fagborun
Consultant Yasmin A. McClinton

Commissioned by Pamela Afram
Editors Sally Beets, Pamela Afram
Designer Brandie Tully-Scott
US Senior Editor Shannon Beatty
Managing Editor Laura Gilbert
Managing Art Editor Diane Peyton Jones
Publishing Manager Francesca Young
Jacket Coordinator Issy Walsh
Production Editor Robert Dunn
Production Controller John Casey
Deputy Art Director Mabel Chan
Publishing Director Sarah Larter

Special thanks to Akua A Boateng, Kariss Ainsworth, Lisa Gillespie, and the rest of the Diversity, Equity, and Inclusion Champions for their invaluable input and support.

First American Edition, 2022
Published in the United States by DK Publishing 1450 Broadway, Suite 801, New York, New York 10018

Text copyright © Taiye Selasi 2022
Copyright in the layouts, design, and illustrations of the Work shall be vested in the Publishers.
DK, a Division of Penguin Random House LLC
22 23 24 25 10 9 8 7 6 5 4 3 2 1
001-326449-Jan/2022

A catalog record for this book is available from the Library of Congress.
ISBN 978-0-7440-4990-9

DK books are available at special discounts when purchased in bulk for sales promotions, premiums, fund-raising, or educational use. For details, contact: DK Publishing Special Markets, 1450 Broadway, Suite 801 New York, New York 10018 SpecialSales@dk.com

Printed and bound in China

FSC | MIX
Paper from responsible sources
FSC™ C018179

This book was made with Forest Stewardship Council ™ certified paper - one small step in DK's commitment to a sustainable future. For more information go to www.dk.com/our-green-pledge

For the curious
www.dk.com